TONY HAWK'S 900 revolution

DROP IN

BY DONNIE LEMKE // ILLUSTRATED BY CAIO MAJADO

VOLUME 1

STONE ARCH BOOKS

a capstone imprint

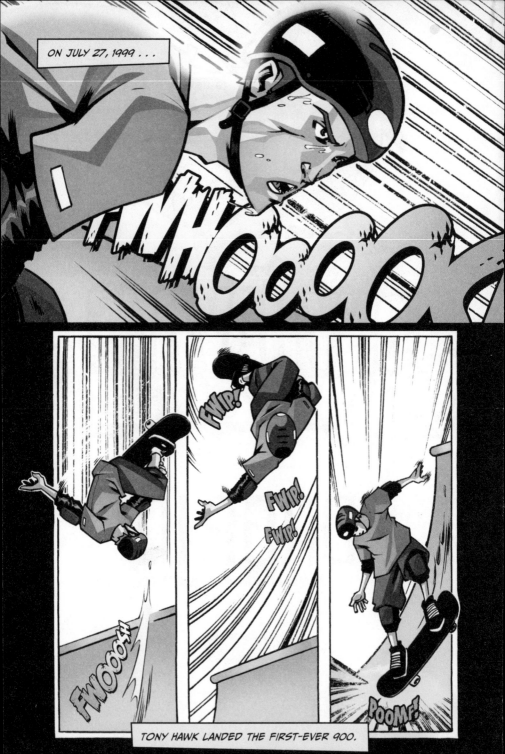

ON JULY 27, 1999 . . .

FWHOOOOK

FWIP!

FWIP!
FWIP!

FWOOOH

POOMF!

TONY HAWK LANDED THE FIRST-EVER 900.

Tony Hawk's 900 Revolution
is published by Stone Arch Books
a Capstone imprint, 151 Good Counsel Drive, P.O. Box 669
Mankato, Minnesota 56002 www.capstonepub.com

Cataloging-in-Publication Data is available on the Library
of Congress website.
ISBN: 978-1-4342-3214-4 (library binding)
ISBN: 978-1-4342-3451-3 (paperback)
ISBN: 978-1-4342-4006-4 (paperback)

Summary: Omar Grebes never slows down. When he's not
shredding concrete at Ocean Beach Skatepark, he's kicking
through surf or scarfing down fish tacos from the nearest
roadside shop. Soon, his live-or-die lifestyle catches the
attention of big-name sponsors. But one of them offers
Omar more than he bargained for . . . a chance to become
the first member of the mysterious 900 Revolution team
and claim his piece of history.

Photo and Vector Graphics Credits: Shutterstock.
Photo credit page 122, Bart Jones/ Tony Hawk.
Photo credit page 123, Capstone/ Karon Dubke.
Flip Animation Illustrator: Thomas Emery
Colorist: Leonardo Lto

Art Director: Heather Kindseth
Cover and Interior Graphic Designer: Kay Fraser
Comic Insert Graphic Designer: Brann Garvey
Production Specialist: Michelle Biedscheid

Printed in the United States of America in Stevens Point,
Wisconsin.
032011
006111WZF11

1

"Bleck! You call this a fish taco?!" shouted Tommy
Goff, spitting out chunks of tortilla and battered sea
bass onto the Imperial Beach Pier. "Where'd you fish it
out of, your toilet?"

"You better watch that mouth, kid!" said the street
vendor in a nearby food truck. The plump, red-faced
cook leaned out of the truck's tiny window and waved
his greasy tongs at the teen.

"Or what?" asked Tommy. "You going to stick me
in your deep fryer? I'd probably taste better than this
garbage." Tommy threw his remaining taco onto the
ground and smashed it through the pier's wooden
planks with his skate shoe.

"Why, you little —!" began the vendor.

Before he finished, the man squeezed back into his truck like an angry turtle into its shell.

"Ha! Thought so," said Tommy. He spun around toward his friend and continued to laugh. "Tell me you recorded that, Omar! I can see the headlines now: 'World's Biggest Chicken serves up World's Worst Fish.' Man, we'll get, like, a billion YouTube hits with that clip."

Omar Grebes looked down at the small, digital camcorder strapped to his palm. The red standby light glowed back at him. "Negative," he replied, pressing the Record button and watching the light turn green.

"Dude!" exclaimed Tommy. "This is exactly what I've been talking about. You want to find a skateboarding sponsor? Then you've got to keep your eyes open. Opportunities don't fall into your lap. They sneak up from behind and hit you like a sack of —"

SPLAT!

A large, black garbage bag struck Tommy in the back of the head, splitting open and covering him in a gooey mess.

Omar quickly raised the camcorder to his eye. Through the lens, he watched tiny bones and pinkish-red slime fall from Tommy's hair. "Fish guts?" he asked his friend, trying to hide a smile.

Tommy's upper lip started to quiver, his nostrils flared, and his eyes narrowed into thin black shadows.

Omar lowered the video recorder. "Uh, you okay, man?" he asked. Although Tommy had played some pretty cruel pranks in the past, Omar had never seen his friend this angry.

For a moment, Tommy stood silent, watching the bloody remains of the food truck's "Catch of the Day" drip off his white cotton tee and onto the skateboard at his feet. "Never better," he finally said.

"In fact," Tommy continued, grasping the bottom of his shirt with both fists and lifting it toward his mouth. "I've been jonesin' for some sushi all day!" He twisted his tee like a wet dishrag, and the thick red liquid spilled onto his smiling face.

"Dude, that's sick!" said Omar, wincing with disgust.

"You know what? You're right," Tommy replied. He spit out the fish juice and wiped his mouth with the cleanest part of his shirt. "You got to be crazy to eat sushi without wasabi!"

"Well, then I guess that nutjob would be all for it!" shouted Omar, pointing over Tommy's shoulder in surprise. The food vendor sprinted toward the boys, swinging another trash bag above his head like a lasso. "And, unless you want seconds, I suggest we *vamos!*"

"Huh?" asked Tommy, puzzled.

"Let's get out of here!" yelled Omar.

The teens hopped on their boards, pushed hard, and quickly left the rabid cook in their concrete wake. They sped down the sidewalks of Seacoast Drive, weaving in and out of palm trees and angry tourists. They ollied off curbs, carved around streetlights, and popped kickflips over waist-high bike racks.

Then, a few blocks away, Tommy skidded to a halt.

"What up?" asked Omar, stopping next to him.

Tommy wiped a sweaty clump of bleached blond hair from his forehead and held out his hand. "Give me it," he ordered.

Omar followed his friend's gaze to the recorder still clutched in his palm. "This?" asked Omar, holding up the digital camera. "Chill out, man. It was funny. You should have seen your face —"

"Funny? We're not out here making cute videos for your friends at Mar Vista High," said Tommy. He swiped the recorder from Omar's hand and punched the Rewind button. "The footy on here is almost enough to get you noticed. Almost."

"Whatever," Omar replied. "You know that tape is airtight."

"Oh, really?" said Tommy.

After a moment, he flipped the recorder's viewfinder toward Omar and pushed Play. Highlights of the day's skate session replayed on the tiny screen.

"What kind of sponsor would shell out for some no-namer poppin' nollies and heelflips down a 5-stair? You gotta go big, Omar, or you ain't going anywhere but home," said Tommy.

"Thanks for the advice, Dad," Omar shot back.

"Man, if your dad was still around," added Tommy, "he'd tell you the exact same thing."

"Yeah, and look where he ended up," said Omar. The teen stared out at the ocean and watched the sun dipping below the horizon. Several surfers had just paddled out, hoping to catch a few glassy waves before dark. Omar imagined his father's final swell. He had to imagine it because he hadn't been there.

Nobody had.

But between police reports, surf reports, and a few tall tales, Omar had pieced together enough information to know that his father's last ride at Killers was a monster. A beast. A fifty-foot behemoth that could smash you into the Baja rocks and then drag you back to the shores of Japan. Omar liked to believe that his father had ended up there — alive and well, a half-world away.

Maybe for the past two years, as Omar had once dreamed, his father had simply been sipping sake, noshing sashimi, and waiting for the perfect wave to ride back home.

But, of course, that wasn't reality. "My dad's dead," said Omar.

"Dude, Zeke is a legend," Tommy replied.

"To who? Your *brahs* at Billy's Board Shop?" asked Omar. "No one east of the I-5 ever gave two craps about him. What makes you think they'll notice me?"

Omar stepped away from his friend and squinted his eyes to get a better look at the nearby surf. He spotted a brown-haired girl wearing a black rash guard and pink bikini bottoms take off on a small roller. She carved across its glassy face in a series of long, slow, arcing turns. Before the wave closed out, she popped her hips and quickly cut back to extend the ride. When the wave finally flattened, the surfer girl dove lazily off her board into the smoldering twilight water.

Omar felt a hand on his shoulder. "Maybe they won't," Tommy whispered in his ear. "But she will."

The teens stared out at the ocean and watched the girl surface. They watched her spit a playful stream of saltwater into the air, shake out her long dreads, and pull at the rash guard that clung to her body like wax.

After a brief moment, the girl grabbed on to her surfboard and started paddling out again.

Omar turned to his friend. "Well, what are we waiting for?" he asked with a smirk.

Tommy held up the video camera and pressed the Record button. "After you," he said, returning the smile.

2

Without hesitation, Omar took off on his skateboard. Tommy followed closely behind, trying hard to keep up and keep Omar in the viewfinder's frame. He wasn't worried about losing him, though. Just like Tommy knew how to change Omar's mind, he also knew exactly where his friend was headed. The two had been tight since before either of them could remember, and by now, Tommy could predict Omar's every thought.

They were practically brothers, after all. Growing up less than three blocks away from each other, the teens had always shared much more than an area code. They shared a love of skateboarding, primo fish tacos, beach bunnies, and punk rock.

In a way, they even shared a father.

When Tommy's dad had bailed on him and his mom, Zeke Grebes took in the boy like a second son. He taught him to skate, to surf, and to be his own man. In return, Tommy watched out for Omar like a big bro, even though he was less than two years older than him. And, now that Zeke was gone, Tommy continued to look after his friend. But to him that didn't mean keeping Omar safe. It meant pushing Omar to the limit. It meant, in the words of Zeke Grebes himself, "Staying radical."

A few blocks later, Omar stopped where the boys had started. At the entrance gate to the Imperial Beach Pier, the skies had darkened, but rows and rows of lights lit up the boardwalk like a runway.

"You back for some more stale fish, bro?" asked Tommy, rolling up alongside his friend and pointing to where he'd smashed his nasty fish taco onto the ground.

"Nah," replied Omar with a smile, "I thought about trying something a little fresher this time."

"What, like *ceviche*?" Tommy joked.

"Not that kind of grindage," said Omar. He snapped his board up to his hand, spun 360 degrees, and then stopped. "More like an Imperial 5-0. What do you think?"

"Ha!" Tommy laughed, but soon noticed Omar wasn't joining in. "Dude, you're not serious, are you?"

"You're the one that said 'Go big, or go home,'" answered Omar. He knew Tommy's allegiance to his own father's words, and, like all younger brothers, Omar tested this devotion whenever possible. "What, too *radical* for you, Tommy?"

"Dream on," his friend replied, scoffing at the suggestion. "I just thought you were too whacked out on energy drinks to even remember that trick."

Omar hadn't forgotten. But it had been the competition, not the caffeine, that had him amped that day three months ago. The teens had been in an all-day, all-out, trick-for-trick skateboarding battle up and down Seacoast Drive. The rules were simple: live or die. Well, at least that's how Tommy and Omar saw it. When one boy threw down a challenge, the other would take it and live on, or die of shame. Of course, like in a heated game of S-K-A-T-E, each player needed the *cojones* to back his own smack. If he couldn't, he lost.

The Imperial 5-0, as the trick had since been nicknamed by the boys, was Omar's final throwdown that day and his first chance to take out Tommy in battle. Despite being a superior skateboarder, Omar had never beaten his big bro.

Like the pros, Omar always skated freakishly clean, but Tommy skated like an adrenaline freak. He would hit any ramp, jump any gap, or grind any rail. More importantly, he knew Omar wouldn't.

To finally win a battle, Omar had decided to flip the switch and turn his greatest weakness into his greatest strength. On that day, he had challenged Tommy to skate the length of the Imperial Pier, 5-0 grind on the safety rail, and return without getting nabbed by beach patrol. Tommy refused. Of course, Tommy hadn't been afraid of the trick — any noob could perform that stunt — and the five-story fall into the churning waters of the Pacific hadn't scared him, either.

Tommy simply wanted to watch his friend punk out.

Since his father's death, Omar hadn't set foot near the ocean, a place that had once been his second home. He had stopped surfing, stopped skimboarding, and couldn't step more than twenty feet onto the pier without tweaking. It wasn't hard for Tommy to predict that Omar's epic trick was bound to be an epic failure. And he was right. On that day three months ago, Omar skated halfway down the pier, and chickened out.

However, today was different. Maybe it was the hottie surfer girl, Tommy's constant nagging, or his fifteenth birthday the next day.

Whatever the reason, Omar was finally ready to take his father's advice and slay his own fifty-foot monster.

"Just keep filming," Omar told Tommy.

"Never stopped," said his friend.

Omar stared at the video camera, and the Record button stared back at him like a stale streetlight. "Time to go," he whispered to himself. Omar sped away, and Tommy followed closely behind.

The boys shot through the entrance gate, passed by the crazed food vendor, and were halfway to the Tin Fish restaurant at the end of the pier in a matter of seconds. Their skateboards clapped loudly over each wooden planks, but Omar barely noticed. His ears tuned to the lapping waves far below. The deep, thunderous crashes echoed the beat of his racing heart.

Omar kept moving.

He pushed harder and harder, ignoring his fears, dozens of "No Skateboarding" signs, and angry strollers along the boardwalk. He didn't look back. He didn't care if Tommy had kept up with him or not. He didn't care if this trick got caught on tape or made his sponsor-me video. This grind would prove something to himself and, better yet, prove Tommy wrong.

Soon, Omar neared the end of the pier and quickly spotted a six-foot section of the wooden safety rail.

Two lamps shined down on the rail like a spotlight.
The edge looked clean, slick, and level enough to grind.
Omar focused. He replayed the motions in his mind,
visualizing a trick he'd executed dozens of times across
ramps, curbs, park benches, and handrails. He picked up
speed, moved his back foot toward the tail of the board,
and tucked in.

Then pop.

Omar ollied high into the air. At the peak of his
jump, just as planned, he locked his back truck onto the
safety rail and began a 5-0 grind across its ledge. For a
moment, everything stopped. He no longer heard the
crashing waves, felt the worry in his gut, or tasted the
uneasy sweat on his lips. He was nine years old again,
grinding the coping on a mini ramp for the very first
time with his proud father looking on. Omar wished he
could hold the trick forever, transform into some kind
of gnarly gargoyle, and become a permanent fixture
on the end of the pier. But his momentum was already
slowing, and Omar prepared to land back onto the
boardwalk and back into reality.

Just then, Omar heard a loud screech overhead. The
sound made him glance toward the darkened sky. A
large black-and-brown bird swooped past his head like a
kamikaze jet, nearly clipping Omar's left ear.

The brief encounter was enough to kill Omar's concentration and knock him from his perch. Suddenly, he was falling and all his senses came flooding back. The waves thundered in his ears, stomach acid burned in his throat, and a helpless scream burst from his lips.

Like all skaters, Omar had taken a couple hits, fractured some bones, and picked up a few battle scars. Still, as the dark ocean water quickly approached, Omar realized that rising from this fall would require some kind of miracle.

Then everything went black.

3

Moments later, Omar felt himself floating again, but he was no longer in the air. When his eyes opened, he was deep beneath the sea. The saltwater didn't sting, and somehow, his bones didn't ache. Like a fetus in the womb, he felt comforted by the isolation, the warmth, and the weightlessness. He wasn't breathing anymore, but he wasn't holding his breath either. Omar scanned his surroundings. He searched for something to indicate if he was dead or alive.

Far below, on the ocean floor, Omar spotted a glowing green dot. At first, it appeared to be nothing more than speck of luminescent plankton, but as Omar swam closer and closer, the object grew larger and larger.

The glowing green light throbbed like a radioactive beacon. Omar could feel its energy pulsate into his toes and out of his skull. He thought about turning back, fearing the object was some sort of alien meteorite or hazardous nuclear waste, but the neon light lured him in like a powerful magnet.

When he was only a few feet away, Omar recognized the object in front of him. There, on the ocean floor, resting amongst sea urchins and thousand-year-old coral, sat the wheel of a skateboard. Under different circumstances, Omar might have questioned the absurdity of this find. At that moment, however, his very presence seemed like something out of a very bad dream. So instead, Omar simply reached down and attempted to grab the wheel from its resting place.

Suddenly, the bulbous head of a snake lashed out from beneath a nearby rock. It lunged at Omar's hand again and again with its long, venomous fangs.

As Omar quickly backed away, the snake slithered toward the glowing green light with hungry eyes. The deadly reptile unlocked its jaw and prepared to swallow the skateboard wheel in one massive gulp. But it never got the chance. The black-and-brown kamikaze bird that had knocked Omar from the pier streaked down through the water.

The bird snatched the wheel from the ocean floor, and darted back toward the surface.

Omar watched the bird disappear, and then stared back down at the snake in disbelief. It continued slithering toward him, hissing angrily and swinging its head from side to side. Omar tried desperately to move, but he couldn't. He felt a heavy weight pressing again and again against his chest, holding him down, not allowing him to escape. The snake slithered closer and closer. It opened its jaws wider and wider, tensed its body, and then struck at Omar's face.

"GAAAAAH!" Omar screamed, hacking up water, gasping for air, and swinging his arms like a prizefighter.

"Dude!" said a voice above him, but Omar kept swinging, screaming, and struggling for air. His body ached, his lungs burned, and his nostrils stung. "Dude, chill out!" the voice said a second time.

Finally, Omar opened his eyes, half expecting a snake to be hanging from his bottom lip. Instead, through his blurry vision, he saw a young woman hovering over him like an angel. Omar immediately recognized her long caramel dreads, black rash guard, and pink bikini bottoms.

"Surfer girl," he whispered to himself.

"Who?" the girl asked.

"Um," Omar hesitated. Tommy had been right. Well, sort of. The trick had certainly gotten the girl's attention and, even though his body was on fire, Omar tried to stay cool. "Is this h-heaven?" he mumbled.

"Very funny," replied the girl, wiping Omar's mouth-to-mouth spit from her lips. "You could have been killed, you know? What kind of stupid stunt were you trying to pull, anyway?"

"An Imperial 5-0," answered Omar.

"A what?" asked the puzzled girl.

"Never mind. My bro and I were just —" Omar stopped. He sat up and finally took a look at his surroundings. Somehow, he had managed to survive the fifty-foot fall and ended up on the beach more than a dozen blocks away. To his right, Omar could see the pier in the distance. Dozens of red and blue police car lights twirled near its entrance gate. Flashlights and spotlights scanned the dark surf below for a missing teenage body.

"Some bro," said the girl, following Omar's gaze. She stood up, grabbed her surfboard, and prepared to leave. "You know, you probably shouldn't stick around here. When they don't find anything beneath the pier, they'll start working their way down the beach."

"Of course," Omar agreed. He struggled to his feet, wiped sand from his faded T-shirt, and fished seaweed from the pockets of his cargo shorts. Then, the disheveled teen began searching the beach for his missing skate shoe. "Well, I guess I'll see you around," he added, playing it cool and not lifting his head.

"Look," said the girl after a moment. "I live a couple houses down. My dad's at work. If you want, you could come hang there for a while, and, like, dry off and stuff."

"For real?" asked Omar, looking up with surprise.

"Yeah, you know," said the surfer girl, "on account of me feeling sorry for you and all."

"So this is just a pity invite, huh?" asked Omar, hesitating slightly and then examining his shameful state. "I'm cool with that."

The surfer girl rolled her eyes, turned, and started walking up the shoreline toward Seacoast Drive. As Omar followed, he spotted a black-and-gray tattoo on the girl's leg. The strange vision he'd nearly forgotten about came rushing back to him. The wheel, the bird, and there, spiraling down the back of the girl's left thigh, was the inky image of that nasty snake. Its jaw opened at the bend in her knee, and each time the girl stepped, the serpent snapped its angry fangs open and closed, open and closed, open and closed.

"See something you like?" asked the surfer girl, catching Omar leering at her backside.

"Nah, I mean, yeah — I mean, I wasn't," Omar stammered. He wanted to ask the girl about her tattoo. He wanted to tell her about his crazy, out-of-whack, tripped-out vision and how her ink was giving him some pretty gnarly flashbacks. But he didn't. "Uh, what did you say your name was?" he said instead.

"I didn't," replied the surfer girl. She walked to the top of the beach, bent down, and pulled a vintage longboard out from behind a row of bushes. Then she looked back again. "But it's Neelu."

Omar hobbled beside her and extended his hand. "Nice," he said with a cocky smile. "I'm Omar, by the way."

Neelu placed the longboard into his open hand. "Looks like you could use this more than me," she said, pointing down at Omar's missing shoe. A limp tube sock hung from his toes like a sloppy piece of toilet paper. "Just try not to fall, okay?"

4

As the girl started north up Seacoast Drive, Omar placed the longboard on the ground and hopped on. The old deck bent slightly under his body weight, and Omar could feel the soft, natural wood beneath his one naked heel. He kicked out, and began to glide smoothly down the sidewalk like a glassy wave. It was the closest Omar had come to real surfing in a really long time.

"Say, Neelu," Omar began, rolling up next to the girl. "How come I've never seen you at Mar Vista?"

"Probably 'cause I don't go to school there," she replied bluntly.

"Oh, right. That's cool," said Omar. "I got a lot of friends who've dropped out. I thought about bailing myself one of these days."

"For what?" asked Neelu. "You planning a career at the In-N-Out Burger or something?"

"No, actually, I was hoping to become a —" Omar started to explain. Then he saw Neelu take a sudden right onto Citrus Avenue. Omar quickly bent his knees, pressed his toes into the edge of the board, and tried carving sharply around the corner after her. The longboard responded, but not as quickly as Omar had expected. He flailed his arms wildly, bounced off the curb, and nearly lost his balance.

A few feet away, Neelu had stopped in front of a small white bungalow. She had seen the entire wretched scene, and stared at Omar like some pathetic noob. "Yes?" she asked with a smirk.

"— a professional skateboarder," whispered Omar, wishing he hadn't had to finish that sentence.

"BAHAHAHA!" Neelu let out gut-busting belly-laugh, waking every dog from Tijuana to Chula Vista.

"Well, at least I'm not a dropout!" Omar shot back. "I was just trying to make you feel better, you know?"

"I didn't drop out," replied Neelu. She started up the driveway of the bungalow. "I'm homeschooled."

"Seriously?" asked Omar. He followed her onto the stoop and leaned the longboard against the side of the house. "Are your parents in a cult or something?"

"Not quite," she said.

Neelu unlocked the front door, stepped inside, and flicked on the lights. Omar walked in after her and nearly collapsed. Surfing artifacts and memorabilia covered every inch of the tiny, twelve-by-twelve foot room. A hundred years of surfboards — from Hawaiian hardwoods to three-fin thrusters — hung horizontally from the floor to the ceiling of each wall. They had been signed by some of the greatest surfers to ever rip, including Kelly Slater, Tom Curren, Larry Bertleman, and even the Duke himself.

"Awesome," whispered Omar, spinning 360s on his heels, trying to take in each and every item.

"Yeah, my dad's a bit extreme," explained Neelu, leading Omar toward the laundry room. "But I'm sure you can relate to that, huh?"

"Nah, my old man passed away," said Omar.

"Oh, right, I'm sorry —" Neelu began.

"That's cool. You didn't know," Omar assured her. "He would have freaked over all of this stuff, though."

Following Neelu through the living room and into a hallway, Omar browsed the continuing collection of mint-condition boards: a 1961 Velzy, a 1978 Mark Richards, a 1982 McCoy, and there, at the very end of the hallway, stood a 1965 Greg Noll Slot Bottom.

Towering nearly ten feet tall, the turquoise-green gun stretched from within inches of the ceiling to within inches of the floor. A massive board for monster waves. "Actually, he had a board just like this," Omar added. "His favorite."

"Only the best," said Neelu.

"He called it his killer, you know," added Omar. He reached out and ran his fingers up and down the board's familiar wood grain center stripe. The crusted salt sticking to the corners of his eyes suddenly made them start to water. "I guess he was right about something."

Omar let out a nervous laugh and then turned. Neelu stood behind him, holding a pair of oversized board shorts and a baby blue polo shirt. "Sorry," Omar said, wiping at his eyes. "I didn't mean to —"

"These should fit," interrupted Neelu, holding out the clothes and trying to avoid the subject. "You can change in the laundry room, if you want." She pointed toward a door on the other side of the hallway.

Without saying another word, Omar took the clothes, entered the laundry room, and shut the door behind him. For the first time that night, he was alone. And, like a ground swell from a distant storm, Omar could feel a wave of deep, distant emotions building inside of him. The room started spinning and shaking.

Two years of anger, sadness, and fear was about to come crashing down, and Omar was riding directly in the impact zone. He quickly stumbled to the nearby window, flung it open, and let out a violent scream.

A cool, Pacific breeze comforted Omar and dried the tears that now spilled down his cheeks. They were the first tears since his father's death. The funeral hadn't even brought them out. But for some reason — maybe the accident, the vision, or the board — Omar felt different somehow, as if his life were about to change.

"Is everything cool in there?" asked Neelu from outside the laundry room door.

For a moment, Omar had forgotten where he was and wondered if the hottie surfer girl had heard him screaming like a wuss.

"Totally," he answered as calmly as possible. Then Omar quickly pulled off his crusty T-shirt and slipped on the baby blue polo. "Just a sec." He removed his belt. He emptied the contents of his cargo pockets onto the washing machine and started taking off his shorts.

"Omar! Open up!" shouted Neelu frantically. She pounded several times on the door, and then burst into the room, slamming the door behind her.

"Whoa!" exclaimed Omar. He quickly pulled up his shorts and zipped his fly.

"I'm not that kind of guy —" he joked.

Neelu pushed her hand over Omar's mouth. He could feel her palm shaking against his lips. "Shut up," she whispered nervously. Then she leaned toward the door, stopped, and listened.

Another door slammed closed on the other side of the house. Omar heard what sounded like footsteps in the living room.

Neelu spun around, grabbed Omar by the collar of the polo shirt, and pulled him close. "You have to get out of here," she said.

"Why?" asked Omar, shocked by the sudden turn of events. "Who is that?"

"My father," Neelu replied.

"Dude, don't worry about it. I'm great with parents," said Omar. He reached toward the handle of the laundry room door.

"No!" shouted Neelu, slapping his hand away. "I mean, not yet, Omar. I shouldn't have brought you here. You have to leave."

"What? How?" he asked. "In case you haven't noticed, we're kind of stuck in this room."

Neelu released one of her hands from Omar's collar and pointed toward the open window behind him. "Take the longboard," she said.

Omar thought about arguing with the girl, but she looked like he had felt only moments before. Neelu wasn't going to budge.

Omar moved toward the window, and then looked back. "By the way, in case I don't see you again, thanks for saving my life," he said. He leaped onto the windowsill and started lowering himself into the backyard.

"Omar!" he heard the girl call after him.

Neelu came to the window, leaned out, and grabbed Omar by the collar again. "You will," she said. "And you're welcome."

Neelu pulled his face toward hers, and their lips touched for the second time that night. A half-second later, when she let go, Omar fell to the ground with a thud. He stared back up at her, dazed, hypnotized by the brown-haired bunny. If their first kiss had brought him back to life, this one had knocked him on his butt.

"Now git!" Neelu whispered down at him.

5

Without hesitating, Omar stood and hobbled around to the front of bungalow. An old-time VW van was now parked in the driveway. Vintage surfboards were strapped atop the green and white relic. Omar crept onto the stoop. He grabbed Neelu's longboard from where he'd left it, and then started back down the stairs.

Just then, through a small opening in the window blinds, Omar saw the back of a man standing in Neelu's living room. He wore a pair of oversized board shorts, like the ones Omar had nearly changed into, and had a large tattoo on his right calf. Omar crept closer to get a better look. Pressing his nose to the window and squinting his eyes, the black-and-gray ink suddenly became much clearer.

An owl? Omar thought, staring at the wide-eyed bird. The predator's wings stretched above the man's knee and its talons nearly scraped against his ankle. Within its clutches, the owl strangled a long checkered snake, which writhed and wrapped its wicked tail around the man's sandaled foot. The man turned and the bird disappeared, replaced by a pale shin moving toward the window.

"Time to ditch this *cult*-de-sac," Omar said to himself. He leaped from the stoop, threw the vintage longboard beneath his feet, and landed on the driveway in one smooth sequence. He pushed hard and didn't look back. Soon, Omar was rolling down Seacoast Drive and halfway back to the Imperial Beach Pier.

Several squad cars still surrounded its entrance gates and dozens of gawkers had stopped, hoping to catch a glimpse of a body washing ashore. Omar knew they wouldn't get that twisted luxury. He also knew he couldn't risk being recognized by witnesses.

Omar made a quick left onto Elm Avenue. Then, starting to groove with the longboard, he carved right onto Second Street and sped toward his house near Reama Park. On the way, he skated past Tommy's place, and spotted a light coming from his friend's bedroom window in the basement.

Two hours had ticked by since they'd last seen each other, and Omar figured Tommy would be worried sick. After all, he didn't even know if Omar was alive.

Omar grabbed the longboard off the ground and crept toward the open window. As usual, he planned to avoid crazy Mrs. Goff and slip into the basement unnoticed. As he approached the house, however, Omar heard his friend arguing with someone.

"Great," Omar said to himself. "Looks like Tommy and his mom are fighting again."

Omar considered turning back, but then he thought he heard Tommy say his name. Omar crept closer. He kneeled near the basement window, placed the longboard against the side of the house, and listened.

"Dude, I told you already!" he heard Tommy shout. "He's gone . . . at the bottom of the sea."

Omar peeked in the basement window. Tommy hadn't been arguing with his mother. He was talking on a cell, pacing back and forth from one end of the room to the other. "What else do you need me to do?" he continued to shout. "What else do you want from me?!"

Omar heard the longboard starting to tip, sliding and scraping against the side of the house. He reached out, trying desperately to snag it and avoid blowing his cover, but the deck fell to the ground with a loud thud.

"Who's there?!" exclaimed Tommy, moving toward the window.

Omar grabbed the board, turned, and started walking away.

"Yo, Omar?!" Tommy yelled after him. "Is that you?"

Omar stopped and glanced back over his shoulder. "Oh, hey, man!" he said, faking surprise. "I didn't know if you'd be home."

"How — I mean — what are you doing here, bro?" asked Tommy, seemingly caught off guard by his unexpected visitor.

Omar turned and started walking back toward the basement window. "Is that any way to greet a guy who's just come back from the dead?" he asked.

"Must have been yuppie hell," joked Tommy, spotting Omar carrying the vintage longboard and wearing a polo shirt for the first time. "Love the color, though. Baby blue?"

"It's a long story —" Omar began.

"What, you have somewhere you got to be? I'm not keeping you from a tennis match or anything, am I?" replied Tommy with a laugh.

"Bite me," Omar shot back, setting down the longboard again, and then slipping through the small basement window.

"Dude, I thought you were dead!" said Tommy, finally greeting his friend with a punch on the shoulder. "I mean, that was some fall."

"Yeah, tell me about it," said Omar. "Actually, I kind of thought you'd be out searching for me — or at least waiting for my body to wash up on shore like the rest of those whackos."

"Yo, didn't you see all those cops out there? You'd think they were handing out free donuts or something," replied Tommy. "You know I can't risk another run-in with the police."

Omar knew all about Tommy's troubles. His big bro had been in and out of juvie since grade school. Drugs, petty theft, assault, and even arson charges had landed him in the kiddie clink a half-dozen times or more. Luckily for Tommy, Omar's father, Zeke, had always been around to bail him out.

From the looks of the basement, however, his friend had since reverted to some of his old ways. Against the far wall, Omar spotted three touch-screen monitors, an ultrathin wireless keyboard, and a juiced-up gaming computer. In his hand, Tommy held a high-tech satellite phone, something Omar had only seen in the glass display cases at RadioShack.

"Who were you just talking to?" asked Omar.

"What? No one," he replied. "I'm the only one here."

"I heard you, Tommy," said Omar. "On the phone. I heard you talking about me. About the accident."

"No — I mean, well, yeah," Tommy explained. "I've been calling around about you, Omar. I thought maybe someone would have seen you, bro. You know, been able to tell me if you were all right."

"Like who? Brody? Rico?" asked Omar. "They the ones that lifted that sat phone for you?"

Tommy looked at the high-tech phone in his hand and then back at Omar. "What? This?" he said, flustered by the sudden accusation. "Oh, I picked this baby up in Tijuana a few weeks ago. Talked the guy down to thirty bucks. Looks real, don't it? Yeah, well, it doesn't work for crap."

Omar pointed at the 50-inch computer monitors on the far wall. "Must've been tough smuggling those across the border, though, huh?" he added.

Tommy glanced in the direction his friend was pointing. "Yeah, strapped them to the moped, right?" he said, letting out a nervous laugh and pretending to rev the accelerator on his dusty old motorbike. Then he moved toward the high-tech equipment and placed his hand on one of the displays. "Nah, man, these are the real deal — fully loaded and fully paid for."

"Where did you ever get that kind of money?" asked Omar, scoffing at his friend's explanation.

"Not me," answered Tommy. "*Us.*"

"Dude, I'm not throwing down for this junk," Omar exclaimed.

"You don't understand," said Tommy. "This stuff is ours. Free and clear. You don't have to pay a dime."

"Sure, Tommy," said Omar. "You and I both know that we ain't getting nothing in this world for free."

"Not free," Tommy replied. "Think of this stuff as an advance. People out there want a piece of you, Omar — a piece of your talent — and they'll pay for it. They gave me this equipment to cut your sponsor-me tape. You know, finally get it out there and get it noticed."

"Who's 'they'?" asked Omar, still skeptical.

"Don't worry about it, bro. Just get me some more of that gnarly footage, and everything else will fall into place. Oh, and speaking of falling," Tommy began with a laugh. He leaned down and pressed a button on the ultra thin, wireless keyboard. Suddenly, the tape of that day's skate session simultaneously appeared on the three monitors, paused to the exact moment Omar had lost his balance and began to fall from the pier. "What do you say tomorrow we give that Imperial 5-0 another shot? You know, 'go big or go home.'"

Omar turned and walked toward the basement window.

"Wait!" Tommy shouted after him. "Where are you going?"

"Home!" replied Omar. "You've got to be crazy if you think I'm trying that trick again!"

"But, dude, you were so close," said Tommy. "You can't give up now. This could be your big break. I mean, if your dad was still around, he would have told you —"

For the second time that night, a wave of emotions flooded Omar's mind. He rushed at Tommy with a clenched fist, but stopped just short of hitting him.

"Shut up, Tommy! Shut up!" Omar shouted, cocking his fist again and again. "Say one more word about my father, and I swear . . ."

"Chill," said Tommy, knowing his friend didn't have the guts to hurt him. "I just meant, not many people get a second chance to slay their own dragon."

"Yeah, and not many people survive a fifty-foot fall, either," said Omar. "If I didn't know better, I'd think you wanted me dead."

Omar lowered his fist and started back toward the window. Without saying a word, he slipped outside, grabbed the longboard from the side of the house, and made his way toward the sidewalk.

"Omar!" Tommy called after him.

Omar stopped but didn't turn.

"He was my father too," said Tommy.

Omar slapped the longboard onto the concrete and hopped aboard. After a brief moment, he turned back toward his friend, who was staring out from the basement window.

"No, he wasn't," Omar finally said. Then he pushed hard and took off down Second Street.

ELCOME COURAG
SNOW KEY TRUS
MPERIAL BEAC
GREBES BROTHER
TIDAL WAVE ZEK
VISIONS SURFIN
REVOLUTION NEEL

6

Omar rolled past the next few blocks wishing he could take back the words he'd just said. Maybe Tommy was right. Maybe he had survived the five-story fall for a reason. Maybe his father would have told him to give it another shot. After all, what other chance did he have to get noticed? How else would he get himself and his mother out of this godforsaken town?

As Omar approached his house, a pair of high beams suddenly lit up near his driveway. *Whose car could that be?* Omar wondered. He knew his mother wouldn't be getting home this late. She should already be inside, worried sick about her precious little boy.

Omar stopped and squinted, trying to get a better look.

Through the blinding light, he spotted the shadows of several objects on top of the oversized vehicle.

Surfboards, Omar thought, suddenly recognizing the vehicle from earlier that night. *Uh-oh.*

Before Omar could even react, he heard the Volkswagen's wheels start to squeal on the asphalt and saw the headlights coming toward him. Omar quickly pressed his right foot onto the back of the board and spun 180 degrees. Facing the opposite direction, he started pushing hard and fast back down Second Street, but the van wasn't stopping. The driver barked on the horn and revved the engine. Soon, the VW was nipping at his heels like an angry dog.

Omar bent low and dug his heels into the left edge of the board. The longboard turned sideways, and its wheel skidded perpendicular to the road. Omar leaned back and put his hand down for balance. His palm scraped against the pitted concrete, but he managed to stay upright and — except for a little road rash — he came out of the turn unscathed. The chase, however, was far from over. The VW screeched into the alley as well, tossing one of the surfboards as it came around the corner on two wheels.

Omar pushed through the alleyway, weaving in and out of cars, dumpsters, and potholes.

Then, on the far side of the alley, he spotted a bright
yellow speed bump. He didn't hesitate. Omar rushed at
the foot-high hop without fear. He pushed harder and
harder and bent so low his butt scraped the board. Then
pop. Like earlier that night, he launched his board into
the air, and ollied the 60-inch plank over the bump with
ease.

He landed on Evergreen Avenue. Cars, buses, and
motorcycles whizzed past him at fifty miles per hour.
Drivers honked their horns and screamed out their
windows at the crazy kid. Omar didn't stop. He laid
into the asphalt, pushing harder, and speeding through
oncoming traffic like a slalom course. Then he carved
another quick right turn and circled back toward
Second Street and his house.

Even though he couldn't hear the van anymore,
Omar didn't look back. He snatched the longboard
off the ground, hopped his front gate, ran over the
lawn, and rushed inside. Slamming and locking the
door behind him, Omar fell onto the entryway floor in a
sweaty heap. For now, his troubles were behind him —
well, at least that's what he thought.

"And just where have you been, young man?" Omar
heard his mother say before he even looked up. "Do you
know what time it is?"

Omar glanced at the clock hanging in the living room. It read 12:02. Even on the weekend, that was way past his curfew. "Time for some birthday cake?" joked Omar, trying to lighten the situation.

Standing at the top of the stairs, his mom cracked a tiny smile, but then quickly straightened her face and folded her arms across her chest. "Not funny," she said sternly. "Now, get to your room! We'll talk more about this in the morning."

Omar didn't say another word. If he played it cool, his mom might let him off easy. He tucked the vintage longboard under his arm and walked slowly up the stairs.

"Where'd you get the board?" his mom asked as he passed her.

Reaching the second floor, Omar turned and looked back at his mother. "A girl — I mean, a friend," he stammered.

"A *girlfriend?*" his mother teased.

"Goodnight, Mom," said Omar, avoiding the question by heading into his bedroom and closing the door behind him.

Inside his bedroom, Omar dropped the longboard onto the floor and crashed face first onto his bed. He couldn't remember the last time he'd been so exhausted.

"If this is fifteen," Omar said to himself, "sixteen must be a nightmare."

A few breaths later, Omar drifted off to sleep and into the first of many dreams. His underwater vision played backward and forward, again and again. The diving bird, the snake, the glowing wheel, all swirled in his head like an underwater whirlpool. And then, she was there. Surfer girl. She smiled at him, flicked her caramel-brown dreads, turned away, and the tattoo on her right thigh came alive. The black-and-gray snake swirled up her leg, around her abdomen and her throat. The evil reptile struck at her again and again, eating her bit by bit, piece by piece, from her skull to her toes. And when it was done, it slithered away, leaving only a bloody stain on the sandy shore. Omar rushed to its side. He grabbed at the scarlet granules of sand, trying to kiss them as they fell through his fingers. And then, from far offshore, Omar heard someone calling his name, speaking to him in Japanese. The words sounded familiar, but he couldn't understand them. And when Omar looked up, he saw Tommy riding a monster wave atop a 1965 Greg Noll Slot Bottom. He cut back and forth, and the swell grew bigger and bigger. The beast towered above him like a midnight dragon and then, an instant later, came crashing down.

Wham!

"Ah!" cried Omar, reaching up and grabbing at a sudden pain on his forehead.

When he removed his hand, a sliver of blood trickled down his palm and through his fingers. Omar looked around. He wasn't at the beach anymore. Tommy, the snake, and the surfer girl weren't there, either. It was just him, alone on the bedroom floor, and more confused than ever.

"A dream," Omar said to himself. He spotted a small speck of blood on the corner of his nightstand, and then pressed his fingers against his aching forehead again. "It was all just a dream!"

Omar pulled himself off the floor and raced into the hallway. From the top of the stairs, he could smell bacon and eggs cooking in the kitchen. On any other day, Omar would have considered that another strange event, but today was his fifteenth birthday. His mother always made something extra special for her only son.

"Mom, you'll never believe the dream I had last night," started Omar, reaching the bottom of the stairs and walking into the kitchen.

As predicted, his mother stood in front of the stove, frying up a pan full of greasy goodness.

Sitting at the kitchen table, however, was someone he never imagined he'd see again.

Surfer Girl.

"Omar, we have a visitor," said his mother, pointing
her spatula toward Neelu and smiling politely. "I assume
this is the friend you were talking about last night?"

For a moment, Omar didn't say a word.

"You hurt your forehead," said Neelu.

Omar stood in the doorway, debating whether to
take a seat or turn and run. "What are you doing here?"
he finally asked the girl. "Are you stalking me, too?!"

"That's no way to greet a guest!" said his mother.

"It's all right, Mrs. Grebes," said Neelu, standing
up from the kitchen table. "I should probably be going
anyway." The girl reached into her satchel and pulled
out Omar's wallet. "Just thought you might need this.
Got your address off the school ID inside."

"Wasn't that thoughtful, Omar?" his mother chimed in. "I think you owe someone an apology."

As Neelu walked past him toward the front door, Omar felt somehow drawn to the girl. She had saved his life, given him his first and second kiss, and died in his dream. Still, he couldn't bring himself to ask for her forgiveness. He watched the surfer girl walk out the front door, and then close it behind her.

"What was that all about?" said his mother.

Omar took a seat at the table. "Don't ask," he replied.

His mother placed a plate in front of her son. Then she grabbed the frying pan and started dishing out scrambled eggs for him. "Omar," she said with a slight hesitation. "Maybe we should have a little talk —"

"Mom!" Omar interrupted, slamming his head onto the table with embarrassment and spilling a pile of mail onto the kitchen floor. "I'm fine, Mom! I'm not like Tommy. There's nothing to worry about." Omar lifted his head and started picking up the spilled envelopes, bills, and second notices. On top of the pile, he spotted a letter addressed to him. "What's this?" he asked.

His mother placed two strips of bacon on Omar's plate and took a quick glance at the envelope. "I thought my big boy wanted his privacy," she answered.

Omar gave her an annoyed glare.

"Must've come in the mail this morning," she continued. "Maybe it's a birthday gift from your grandma."

"Nice!" said Omar. He ripped open the end of the envelope and gave it a quick shake, half expecting a scribbly twenty-dollar check from his grandmother to spill out. Instead, a small white note card fell onto the kitchen table. On the front of the card, the words THE REVOLUTION had been typed in bold red letters.

Omar flipped the card over, and on the back he read a simple message:

"Congratulations, Mr. Grebes. You have been chosen to ride for us. Our offices are located on the corner of Evergreen and Atwood. Please stop by at your earliest convenience for more information.

— Eldrick Otus."

"Dude!" Omar exclaimed, leaping up from the kitchen table and spilling his plate of bacon and eggs onto the ground. "Do you know what this means?!"

"Yeah, now I have to clean the floor," answered his mother.

"Forget about that, Mom," said Omar, holding out the card and beaming with pride. "You may never have to clean another floor again — not here and definitely not at that crappy job of yours."

"That job puts food on this table," she replied, and then spotted Omar glancing down at the spilled breakfast. "And don't even say it, young man. I'm not in the mood for your jokes."

"I'm serious. Just look," Omar said, handing the card to his mother. "Someone wants to sponsor me, Mom. *Me*! Can you believe it? This is what I've been working for. All those bruises and broken bones. All those late-night sessions. It's finally going to pay off!"

"How?" asked his mother.

"Thanks for the vote of confidence, Mom," said Omar.

"No, I didn't mean it like that, Omar," she explained. "I just meant how did they find out about you?"

Omar snatched the card back from his mom, giving it a second look. "Not sure," he replied. "Maybe Tommy sent them my sponsor-me tape. I didn't think it was finished yet, but he probably sent copies out without telling me. Typical Tommy, you know?"

"Be careful, Omar," said his mother, still sounding skeptical. "I mean, there's a lot of scams out there."

"What? Like that slap chopper thing you bought online?" said Omar, pointing at a dusty gadget on the kitchen counter. "I'm not going to fall for some slick salesman."

"I know," his mother replied. "It's just — well, you can't trust anyone these days."

"Okay, Mom," said Omar, rolling his eyes and walking out of the kitchen. "I got to call Tommy. Maybe someone around here will be excited for me —"

"Omar!" his mother shouted after him.

The teen turned and looked back at his mom, frustrated by her lack of enthusiasm. "What?" he asked.

"Your father would have been proud," she said.

Omar watched a tear fall from the corner of each of his mother's eyes. He knew only one of those tears fell for him. The other fell for his father, who had gone missing exactly two years ago. On a morning just like this one, Zeke had slipped out early to catch a few waves before his son's thirteenth birthday breakfast. Omar and his mother sat at the kitchen table waiting for him to return. They watched his eggs get rubbery and cold, the bacon turn a fatty shade of white, and the coffee stain a ring in his mug. Eventually, Omar's mother stood, exited the kitchen without a word, and started making a few phone calls.

A week later, the food was still there, stinking up the kitchen like a bad memory. The San Diego Police Department, the bros at Billy's Board Shop, and even a private investigator couldn't give her an answer.

"Maybe he just left," some of them had suggested. "You know, got tired of the real world and bolted."

But she couldn't accept that explanation. Wouldn't accept it. Zeke was a decent man, a good husband, and a great father. And, even after the police had declared him dead and the family had spread the ashes of his belongings across the shores of Todos Santos, the uncertainty surrounding his disappearance must have been killing her.

For Omar, however, it kept him alive.

"Thanks, Mom," Omar finally replied. He knew that anything more — a hug, a kiss, or even a simple "Is-everything-all-right?" — could send her spiraling back down that whirlpool of doubt.

Instead, he ran up the stairs, grabbed his cell phone and the longboard from his bedroom, and then dashed out the front door.

"Happy Birthday!" his mother yelled after him. "And don't forget to call me!"

"Thanks, Mom," shouted Omar, starting down the sidewalk on the longboard. "I will!"

8

Riding down Second Street, Omar checked his cell. He knew Tommy would never be up at this time of the morning. Besides, after last night, he figured a warning shot before showing up at his friend's house unannounced couldn't hurt. However, a message scrolled across the phone's display screen: 1 TEXT FROM TOMMY GOFF 12:21 AM.

Omar figured his friend had beaten him to the punch and called to apologize late last night. He clicked Enter on his phone, and the message popped up on the tiny screen:

I AM SORRY OMAR. IT'S NOT ME. IT'S THEM. THEY ARE THE SNAKES OMAR! THEY ARE THE SNAKES!!!!

Omar skidded to a stop in front of Tommy's house. He recalled the vision from the previous day, the black-and-gray tattoos, and the dream. The text message appeared to be a warning, but against what? His friend couldn't have known about any of these events. Omar hadn't told Tommy about the vision, the surfer girl, or her lunatic father.

"Or did I?" he wondered aloud.

Omar sprinted across Tommy's front lawn to the basement window. He rapped on the glass and waited. After a moment, when his friend hadn't answered, Omar peeked inside. Against the far wall of the basement, the monitors, the wireless keyboard, and the high-tech computer were all gone — and so was Tommy.

For a second, Omar considered knocking on the front door and asking crazy Mrs. Goff about her son and the missing equipment. But then again, he thought, maybe this bad situation was actually a good direction. Maybe their little talk last night had finally woken Tommy up. Maybe he had decided to stop lying to himself and return the stolen equipment. Sure, Omar knew his thinking was wishful, but he wasn't about to rat out his big bro before they had a chance to talk.

Omar took off on the longboard, continuing toward the location on the note card in his back pocket.

A few beats later, he arrived at the corner of Evergreen and Atwood. He hadn't remembered a skate shop in the area, and he didn't see one now. Rundown bungalows, rusted-out cars, and chain-link fences lined the sidewalks as far as Omar could see.

Maybe Mom was right, he thought. *Maybe this was all some sort of scam or another one of Tommy's pranks.*

Omar double-checked the directions in his pocket. When he looked back up, he spotted a small concrete building on the opposite side of the street. No bigger than a school bus, the building looked like some kind of 1950s A-bomb bunker, except each and every wall had been tagged from top to bottom with technicolor graffiti.

Omar skated closer. He tried to decipher the bombs, slashes, and scribbles, but like faces in a crowd, the identities of the words and symbols were totally unfamiliar. Then, above the building's front doorway, Omar recognized the bold, blocky letters of one of these straights: T H E R E V O L U T I O N

Omar held up the note card in his hand and quickly compared it with the simple tag.

"This must be the place," he said, confirming the similarities. He grabbed the rusted handle of the front door, paused, and took a deep breath.

During the past twelve hours, Omar had felt caught in the barrel of a wave, unsure if he'd get shacked or come out of this tube ride alive. The next few minutes, however, would almost certainly determine that fate.

Omar stepped inside the bomb bunker and into a whole other world. The rough exterior of the building completely masked the sickest shop Omar had ever seen. Skate decks covered every inch of every wall like some kind of rock star sheetrock. From floor to ceiling hung some of the wickedest woods to ever ride a ramp, including Tony Alva's Dogtown deck, Aldrin Garcia's highest-ollie hardwood, a Chris Cole skateboard, and a Powell-Peralta ripper board signed by the original Bones members.

Browsing the collection, Omar could hardly believe that a hella-cool place like this could fly under his radar. Then again, some of the best skate and surf spots in SoCal were also some of the best-kept secrets. If it wasn't on the DL, any fresh hangout would soon be flooded with kooks, posers, and wannabes.

A million questions raced through Omar's mind, and he scanned the store for an employee to answer them. Instead, near the rear of the shop, Omar spotted a tall pedestal with a glass display case on top, illuminated by a single spotlight from the ceiling.

Omar moved closer and peered into the display. Inside, floating in the middle of the large glass cube, hovered what appeared to be a small shard of plywood, no bigger than a flash drive. Omar leaned even closer, trying to identify the mysterious object, and his warm breath fogged up the glass of the display.

Suddenly, the wooden shard started glowing!

A bright green light burst out of the object in every direction. Omar shielded his eyes with surprise. Then, figuring he had set off some kind of security alarm, Omar quickly grabbed the tail of his t-shirt and wiped his spitty breath off of the display. When his hand brushed against the glass, an electric bolt of energy shot through Omar's body, quivering from the nerves in his hand to the nerves in his toes. Omar couldn't move. His hand stuck to the glass like a magnet. Omar fell to his knees, his body jerking and flailing wildly in a full-on seizure. And then, the visions began again . . .

Like rapid-fire clips in a music video, hundreds of pictures flashed through Omar's mind, but this time the series of images looked somewhat familiar. High atop a half-pipe stood Tony Hawk. Sweating and exhausted and with thousands of fans cheering him on, the Birdman stared down the face of the wicked ramp with a look of pure determination.

After a brief hesitation, he dropped in. He soared from side to side, and then unleashed a vertical vortex. Two and a half rotations. Nine hundred degrees. And when the Hawk finally came back down to Earth, he hoisted his skateboard into the air like a Spartan sword and celebrated his monstrous feat.

Still hypnotized by the visions, Omar suddenly felt a sense of power, courage, and accomplishment course through his veins. Like a spectator, he watched the Hawk lift his 900 deck higher and higher into the air.

But then, a nanosecond later, everything changed.

Omar's warm, fuzzy feelings quickly turned into cold-blooded fear. Tony's skateboard started warping, twisting, and expanding like a violent balloon. Fans and onlookers scattered in all directions, running and fleeing the scene in terror.

Then, *BAM!*

The 900 board shattered into dozens of pieces, leaving only a bright white light behind — and leaving Omar unconscious on the skate shop floor.

9

Moments later, through what sounded like a concrete culvert, Omar could hear his name. "Omar? Omar?" the voice called to him again and again.

Omar slowly opened his aching eyes. He soon recognized his surroundings, but not the person standing over him. The tall, silver-haired man, wearing board shorts and a polo shirt, extended his hand toward the teen. "Welcome to the Revolution, Omar Grebes," he said, offering to help him to his feet.

"Huh?" asked Omar, still a little confused.

"I've been waiting for you," the man continued.

Omar accepted the stranger's hand and pulled himself off the floor. "How did you know my name? I mean, who are you?" he asked.

"Those are two very different questions, Omar,"
replied the man with a smile. Then he bent down and
picked up the note card, which Omar had accidently
dropped onto the floor. "Let's start with the second one.
My name is Eldrick Otus —"

"Mr. Otus!" exclaimed Omar, recognizing the man's
name from the invitation and suddenly feeling a little
embarrassed. "I'm so sorry. It's just — I took this major
spill yesterday, and I haven't been feeling myself since
then, you know? I hope this doesn't ruin my chances
of riding for you or anything."

"Of course not," said the man. "And call me Eldrick."

"Cool," said Omar, feeling a little more comfortable.
"Then I assume you've seen the tape?"

The man nodded. "Yes, we've seen the tape, Omar,"
he replied.

"Great!" Omar exclaimed. "But you should probably
know that the video wasn't finished. I mean, if you
guys are having any doubts about sponsoring me or
anything, I'd totally be down for shredding a little demo
or whatever you need —"

"Perhaps, there's been a bit of a misunderstanding,
Omar," interrupted Eldrick. "We're not interested in
sponsoring you."

Omar felt that barrel of hope begin to close out.

"You're not?" he asked, puzzled.

"No, son," answered Eldrick. "We have other plans for you."

The strange man turned and headed toward the back room from which he'd come. And that's when Omar saw it — the tattoo of an owl stared back at him from Eldrick's calf. The image was unmistakable. The wide eyes. The razor-sharp talons. The tortured snake. He'd seen the whole thing only hours before while peering through the blinds of Neelu's living room window.

Omar needed out of the situation and fast.

As Eldrick exited the room, Omar spun around and turned to run. *WHAM!* Instead, he smashed directly into the display pedestal, which wobbled for an instant and then fell to the ground in a thunderous crash.

Eldrick rushed back into the main room. "Hey!" he shouted angrily. "Where are you going?"

Without hesitating and without thinking, Omar grabbed the small shard of wood out off the shattered display on the floor. The powerful energy returned to his body, but this time it surged through him like a rush of pure adrenaline.

Omar felt alive, unafraid, and unstoppable.

WELCOME TO THE REVOLUTION
STALEFISH

WITH HIS NEWFOUND ENERGY, OMAR RACED DOWN ATWOOD AVENUE, CUTTING IN AND OUT OF TRAFFIC LIKE A RAZOR.

I MUST BE DREAMING.

HIS LINES HAD ALWAYS BEEN TIGHT, BUT THIS WAS INSANE.

LIKE A HIGH-TECH LASER BEAM, OMAR'S EYES SCANNED THE LANDSCAPE IN FRONT OF HIM.

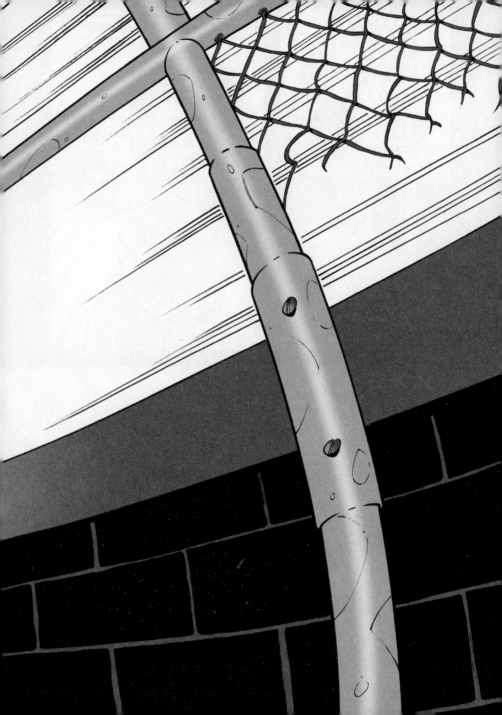

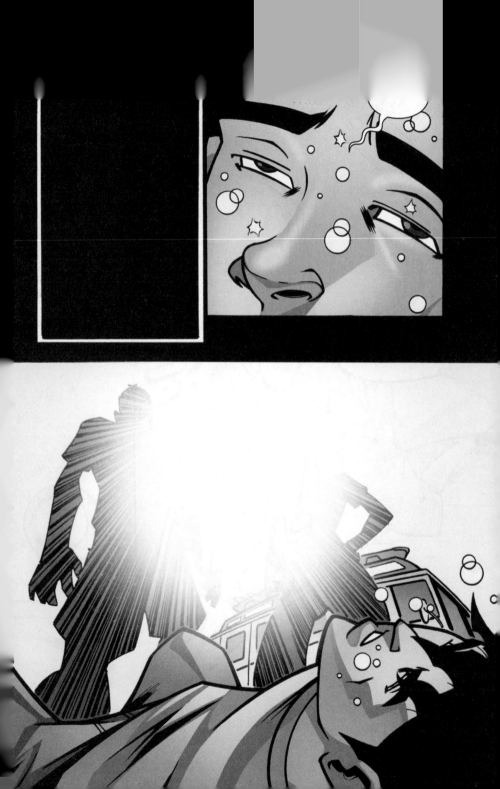

10

A few minutes later, Omar felt a large hand grasp the top of his head, and then yank off a dark hood with a few strands of his hair. Sitting cross-legged in front of him was a man who no longer needed an introduction.

"Eldrick Otus," Omar spit from his bloodied lip.

"Correct," said the man. "And you're Omar Grebes. But I believe we've already established that."

Omar glanced around the van for a way to escape, but instead of windows and doors, dozens of miniature LED monitors lined the interior walls. Videos of teens just like himself played on the display screens. Skaters, surfers, snowboarders, freestyle BMX bikers, and other athletes were all represented.

"What is this? My competition or something?" asked Omar, even more frightened and confused. "Because I can make your decision a little easier. I'm out! There's no way I'm competing for this job."

"You're not here to compete, Omar," answered Eldrick. "You've already been chosen."

"For what?!" shouted Omar.

"The Revolution," replied the man.

"Dude, I don't know what you're talking about," said Omar, "but I think I'll pass. Thanks, though."

Omar rose to his knees and motioned toward the rear double doors of the van. At the same time, he spotted Eldrick reaching into the pocket of his board shorts and half expected him to pull out a knife. Instead, the strange man unveiled the small shard of wood from the skate shop, pulsing with energy.

"Do you know what this is?" Eldrick asked, holding the piece toward the boy.

Omar sat back down, but didn't respond.

"It's called a Fragment," continued Eldrick, answering his own question. "One piece of a very important skateboard."

"Big deal," said Omar. "I've been in your shop. It's probably the sickest collection I've ever seen. You've got dozens of boards."

"None like this," said Eldrick. "Without this board, the others wouldn't even exist. Without this board . . . neither would we."

"Dude, you really are whacked!" said Omar, letting out a gut-busting laugh. "I mean, when Neelu told me she was homeschooled, I figured you must be in some kind of cult, but this is out of control!"

"When did the visions begin, Omar?" interrupted Eldrick.

Omar immediately stopped laughing. "How did you —?" he started, but a nervous bubble rising in his throat made him stop.

"The same way you pulled off that massive feeble grind out there," explained Eldrick. The wooden shard in the man's hand glowed brighter and brighter, and tentacles of electric energy slithered around his wrist and down his arm.

"That?" asked Omar, pointing toward the glowing object. "What? Does it have some kind of superpowers or something?" He let out another nervous laugh.

"We're not exactly sure," answered Eldrick with a straight face. "Only a chosen few can unlock the extraordinary powers within the Fragments."

"Fragments?" repeated Omar. "Like, more than one?"

"Many."

"And where did they come from?" asked Omar, wanting to hear the end of the man's foolish tale.

"I believe you already know," replied Eldrick. He grabbed Omar's wrist and, like a surge of electricity, the Fragment's energy flowed from his hand and into the boy's body. Suddenly, those rapid-fire images of Tony Hawk ripped through Omar's mind once again. With thousands of screaming fans cheering him on, the Birdman dropped in, executed the world's first-ever 900, raised his skateboard into the air in celebration, and then, like a megaton bomb, the deck exploded into a bright white light.

A second later, Eldrick released the boy's hand, and for a moment Omar sat in stunned silence.

"The 900?" the teen finally asked. Omar knew all about this monumental skateboarding trick. He'd been born the day it happened — July 27, 1999 — a fact his father had never let him forget. "What does Tony Hawk have to do with any of this?"

"Everything," answered Eldrick, raising the wooden shard again. "The Fragments are pieces of that board."

"Dude, I'm totally not following you," said Omar, growing frustrated by the situation. "None of this makes any sense!"

"We don't completely understand it either, son," added Eldrick. "But somehow, the 900 opened a sort of portal — a tunnel between two worlds. Some people witnessed that explosion. Others have no recollection of the event. But the Fragments are real, Omar. They exist. Individually, they hold great energy and strength, but together — well, their power is unimaginable."

"But why me?" asked Omar. "Why are you telling me all this?"

"You are one of the chosen few," said Eldrick, pointing at the miniature LED screens surrounding him. "The first of the many Keys who are conduits of this energy, and the only ones who can locate it."

"Okay, fine! Let's go find these so-called Fragments, and get this whole thing over with," replied Omar, hoping to satisfy the madman.

"It's not that easy, son," said Eldrick.

"Of course not," Omar scoffed.

"You see, when the 900 board shattered, the Fragments were scattered across the globe," explained the man. "The whereabouts of these pieces are difficult to determine, at best."

"Yeah, yeah," Omar interrupted. "Why don't you let the 'Chosen One' worry about that, huh?"

"There's more," said Eldrick.

"Others seek the Fragments as well," said the man. "But unlike us, they do not wish to secure and protect this extraordinary power. They plan to unleash it onto the world — and, like snakes, prey on the weakest among us."

Omar's heart started pounding in his chest, beating faster and faster in rhythm with the pulsating shard of wood. Tommy's text message from early that morning suddenly scrolled through his mind like the ticker on a sports broadcast: IT'S THEM. THEY ARE THE SNAKES OMAR! THEY ARE THE SNAKES!!!!

Omar popped to his feet. He plowed into Eldrick like a running back, pushing and shoving his way toward the van's double doors.

"What's wrong?!" Eldrick exclaimed. He grabbed the boy in both arms and tackled him to the floor of the van. "What did I say?"

"Tommy warned me about you!" cried Omar, struggling to free himself from the man's grasped. "He warned me, and I didn't listen!"

"Warned you about what?" asked Eldrick.

"YOU! THE SNAKE!" Omar screamed out. "What have you done with my friend?"

Eldrick followed Omar's gaze toward the tattoo on the back of his calf.

"I can explain, Omar, but you need to calm down," he said, pressing the boy onto the floor again and again. "You've got it all wrong, son."

"Quit calling me that, you freak! I'm not your son!" shouted Omar. "My father is dead!"

"I know all about your father," said Eldrick.

Suddenly, the wall of LED monitors went black and then, after a brief moment, they flicked back on and formed a single, vibrant blue video image. It was the ocean, recorded from high above on some sort of aerial helicopter camera. The roar of a distant wave echoed through the van. The camera pulled out further, revealing a massive swell, throbbing and rippling like the skin of a giant beast. It grew bigger and bigger.

And then, the camera zoomed out even more and, atop the monster's back, a tiny surfer cut back and forth down the face of the wave. Even from this distance, Omar recognized the turquoise gun with the wood-grain center stripe. A 1965 Greg Noll Slot Bottom.

"Where did you get this tape?" shouted Omar.

"Watch," said Eldrick, still holding down the boy.

The massive beast started curling and closing out. The surfer raced toward the bottom of the wave, trying to outrun its foamy fangs. It nicked at the board, and the rider came closer and closer to certain doom.

"Let me go!" Omar screamed, violently flailing his arms and legs. "I'm not going to watch my father die!"

"Just look," Eldrick ordered him again.

Out of the corner display, another surfer sped into the larger picture. He darted toward Omar's father like a bullet, slipped in front of him, and stole ownership of the wave. However, neither Zeke Grebes nor the snake could outrun the killer behind them. The monster wave suddenly closed out, collapsing onto itself and spraying a squall of water a hundred feet into the air.

On the floor of the van, Omar collapsed as well, and a flood of tears spilled from his eyes. Eldrick placed his hand on the boy's shoulder, trying to comfort him the best he could.

"Get off of me! Get off of me!" shouted Omar. "Why would you show me that?! Why does any of this matter?"

As the video continued rolling, Omar heard the hum of a wave runner vibrate through the van's speakers. Then, on the displays and out of the fog of water, the machine appeared, ridden by large man wearing a jet-black wetsuit and scuba tank. The man leaned to the side and extended his hand toward the surface of the ocean. From beneath the surf, another hand appeared, flailing wildly and grasping for help.

The man in black grabbed it, and pulled a teen out of the breaker and onto the waver runner. Alive.

"Tommy," whispered Omar, rubbing his watery eyes in disbelief at sight of his friend. "But I don't understand."

"We don't expect you to, Omar," said Eldrick.

"*We?*" asked the boy.

IMPERIAL BEAC

GREBES BROTHER

TIDAL WAVE ZEK

VISIONS SURFIN

REVOLUTION NEEL

11

Omar hadn't even noticed that the van had stopped until he heard the rear double doors start to open. And there, on the other side, stood Neelu. "I'm sorry, Omar," she said. "I meant to tell you, but it wasn't the right time. That's why I left the card at your house."

"That was you?" asked Omar.

Neelu nodded.

"This is crazy!" Omar cried out. "I mean, you lure me to your shop, kidnap me, show me one stupid video, and what? You expect me to believe that I'm some kind of prophet, that these Fragments are more powerful than nukes, and that the fate of the world lies in my hands. And then, on top of all that, you tell me that my big brother killed my father. Is that about right?"

"Your brother didn't kill him, Omar," Eldrick added.

"Oh, right," Omar shot back, his hands shaking in fear. "It was an evil organization out to rule the world. I mean, how did you even get this tape? Did you piece it together on some kind of home editing software or something? Nice work, man. You're officially smarter than my grandmother, but you're not fooling me!"

Omar pushed passed Neelu, scooted out of the van, and scoped out his surroundings. He didn't recognize the area. They were parked in an abandoned lot, and a hundred feet away near a cliff overlooking the ocean stood a UH-60 Black Hawk helicopter. The blades on the high-tech aircraft spun around and around, whirling faster and faster and priming for takeoff.

Omar felt a hand on his shoulder. He looked back and saw Eldrick standing behind him with a smile on his face.

"We're the eyes in the sky," said Eldrick, pointing toward a high-definition camera mounted on the Black Hawk's landing skids.

Neelu walked to the aircraft, lifted one leg up into the side door, and looked over her shoulder. "So, are you with us?" she yelled back at her friend. Wind from the spinning rotors of the Black Hawk helicopter whipped through her hair and down the back of her rash guard.

The shirt flapped in the breeze and lifted slightly above her waist, just long enough for Omar to spot a second tattoo on the small of her naked back. A falcon. The lightning-fast predator was in a full-on dive, streaking toward that wicked snake on her left thigh.

"Birds of a feather, right, Omar?" added Eldrick, following Neelu into the aircraft and allowing the boy to make his own decision.

Omar's brain was spinning faster than the helicopter blades. Like parts of a skateboarding trick, he tried piecing together the events of the day into something solid and real. The accident. The visions. The Fragment. His father. Tommy. None of it made any sense in his head. So instead of thinking, Omar decided to follow his instincts — as he often did at the skatepark — and continue this gnarly ride.

Before he knew it, Omar was sitting inside the tricked-out heli, flying south across the Pacific Ocean. Inside the cockpit, Eldrick fed the pilot instructions. Neelu fiddled with some high-tech equipment in the rear of the aircraft like some kind of self-taught hacker.

"You were right, Neelu," said Omar, finally finding the courage to speak again. "Your dad is a bit extreme."

Neelu let out a cautious laugh. "Would I lie?" she replied, looking back at her day-old friend.

"Good question," said Omar. "Did you know about my father? Did you know about Tommy?"

"Yes," answered Neelu. "Yes, I knew."

"Then why?" asked Omar. "I've grown up with Tommy my whole life. He was — well, you know — like a brother to me."

Neelu moved toward Omar, kneeled in front of him, and held out a large GPS watch. "Tommy wasn't always one of them," she said, "but at some point they turned him."

"Did my father know?" questioned Omar.

"Have you ever heard the expression 'Keep your friends close, but your enemies closer'?" she asked.

"Of course," he replied, holding out his arm and allowing Neelu to strap the high-tech device to his wrist.

"Well," continued the surfer girl, "your father took those words to heart. He kept Tommy close to protect the Fragments, protect you, and protect all of us. And, until now, he succeeded."

"What do you mean?" questioned Omar.

Eldrick stepped out of the cockpit and into the rear of the aircraft. "She means they're close," he said.

"To what?" Omar asked, hoping he didn't already know the answer to his question.

"Another piece of the board," said Eldrick, confirming those fears.

"Yes, but now we have you, Omar," Neelu added. "You can help us find the Fragment before them and continue your father's legacy."

"But how?" asked Omar. "I don't even know where to begin."

"You will," said Eldrick. He grabbed the handle of the Black Hawk's sliding side door, pulled it open, leaned out, and let the wind rush through his silvery hair. "You will."

Neelu pressed a small red button on the GPS watch, and the gadget on Omar's wrist started beeping. "Don't worry, Omar," she said, leading her friend toward her father and the helicopter's door. "That device will track your location. No matter where the current takes you, we'll be close behind."

Omar glanced outside. On the distant horizon, he spotted the small twin islands of Todos Santos, but directly beneath them, nothing but the churning midnight waters of the Pacific Ocean could be seen.

Omar quickly stumbled away from the door, feeling his hydrophobia suddenly take hold again. "You want me to jump?!" he exclaimed.

"It's the only way," Neelu replied.

"Time is running out," added her father. "Soon, they'll have the Fragment, and we'll all be facing much deeper waters."

"How can I trust you?" asked Omar.

"You can't," stated Eldrick. "From this point forward, the only person you can trust is yourself. But if you're asking for my advice, Omar, follow your instincts . . . and drop in."

Take the challenge or die of shame, Omar thought, considering his options. Less than twenty-four hours earlier, he hadn't backed down from Tommy, and he wouldn't do it today either.

Omar rose to his feet. He glanced at Eldrick and Neelu, and then out at the horizon. "Stay radical," Omar whispered to himself, echoing his father's infamous words.

A moment later, he sprinted toward the helicopter door, and took a leap of faith.

12

Omar fell wildly through the air, uselessly flapping his arms and trying to control an out-of-control dive. Then, as Eldrick had instructed, the young man allowed his instincts to take over again. And soon, like his avian namesake, Omar dove gracefully through the sky like a black-and-brown grebe bird, speeding toward the deadly breakers below.

A split second later, Omar lifted his arms above his head and cut through the surface like a bullet. He darted deeper and deeper, and the waters grew darker and darker. Down, down, down, Omar swam into the abyss until he was skimming along the colorful, jagged coral and passing by surfperch, striped bass, and Chinese mitten crab at the bottom of the sea.

Kicking along the ocean floor, Omar experienced a
tightness in his chest and a caffeinated pressure in his
eyes. Unlike his underwater vision, he no longer felt
like a fetus in a comforting womb; he was a newborn
baby with an undeniable need to breath. Omar wanted
to unlock his lips, open his throat, and let a tidal wave
of saltwater fill his shriveled lungs.

But he didn't.

A far greater force kept his mouth shut, his throat
closed, and the floodwaters at bay. He sensed something
familiar about his surroundings. The warm waters, the
thousand-year-old coral, the spiny black sea urchins,
and there — resting silently on the ocean floor — sat
that glowing green wheel of the skateboard.

As in his vision, the 900 Fragment throbbed like a
radioactive beacon, luring Omar closer and closer like
a powerful magnet. And again, when he was only a few
feet away, Omar reached down and attempted to grab
the wheel from its resting place.

Suddenly, something lashed out from behind a
nearby rock, but instead of the black head of a snake,
the black-gloved hand of a scuba diver struck at Omar
again and again. The masked man wrapped his arms
around the boy, squeezing him, holding him down, and
waiting for him to die.

Omar bucked, wriggled, and writhed, trying desperately to escape the diver's grasp. He kicked wildly and threw his elbows from side to side.

Finally, in one last exhausted flail of his arms, Omar connected. His elbow cracked into the side of the diver's head with a powerful thud, dislodging his scuba mask and sending him floating, unconscious, toward the coral reef below.

Omar didn't hesitate. He streaked down through the water, snatched the glowing wheel from the ocean floor, and darted back toward the surface. The Fragment's incredible energy coursed through his body again. He kicked harder and faster, and soon the shallower waters grew bluer and brighter. *Just a few more feet,* Omar thought, and he would be able to breathe again and be safe inside the UH-60 Black Hawk helicopter.

But then, like a zombie pulling him back into a grave, something snagged Omar's foot from behind. When he looked down, Omar saw a face more frightening than the undead.

It was Tommy.

Omar's neighbor, his best friend, his big bro tugged violently at his foot, trying to pull him back down into the deep dark waters. Tommy had been the one in the scuba mask.

Tommy had been searching for the Fragment as well, and no amount of history, no family connections, no brotherly bonds would stop him from getting it.

With little oxygen remaining in his bloodstream and no other choice, Omar clutched the Fragment tightly in his hand and looked Tommy straight in the face. His best friend's upper lip quivered, his nostrils flared, and his eyes narrowed into thin black shadows.

For a moment, Omar wondered if he could have seen this coming. Had he mistaken the slippery schemes of a snake for brotherhood? Evil manipulations for love? Only one thing was certain: Eldrick had been right. From this point forward, Omar could trust no one but himself.

Without another thought, Omar gave his big bro a swift kick to the brow. Once again, Tommy's lifeless body drifted toward the ocean floor.

This time, however, Omar watched until nothing remained but the deep, midnight waters of the Pacific. Maybe he would see his friend again someday, or maybe the beach patrol at the Imperial Pier would finally find that missing body of a boy.

Either way, Omar knew that nothing would ever be the same.

Then, with a few more kicks, Omar surfaced.

And there, hovering nearby in the Black Hawk heli, were his new friends — his new family — Eldrick and Neelu. They quickly pulled Omar back into the aircraft and set off toward off the horizon.

"Are you okay, Omar?" asked Neelu, wrapping her arms around their hero.

Omar handed her the glowing Fragment. "What now?" he said, avoiding the question.

"Your quest continues," added Eldrick.

"You mean —?" Omar began.

"Yes," Eldrick interrupted. "This is only the beginning. We have many more pieces to find and many more members to recruit."

"But what about my mother?" asked Omar. "I can't just leave her behind."

"Don't worry, Omar," said Eldrick. "We've found someone to take care of her while you're gone."

"Who?" asked Omar.

Neelu gave her friend a knowing smile. "Only the best," she replied, repeating the words she had used to describe that 1965 Greg Noll Slot Bottom hanging on her father's wall.

During the past twenty-four hours, many of Omar's visions had been fulfilled, and he wondered if another dream had finally come true.

But, for now, a little uncertainty was more than enough. "A real legend, huh?" he said.

Neelu nodded.

Omar turned toward the door of the helicopter and gazed outside. The crimson sun began to set on the horizon, but for one SoCal skater — and the rest of the world — a Revolution was rising.

The Beginning.

OMAR GREBES_
CODE NAME: STALEFISH

AGE: 15

HOMETOWN: Imperial Beach, California

SPORT: Skateboarding

INTERESTS: Punk, Food, and Girls

BIO: An active fifteen-year-old boy, Omar Grebes
never slows down. When he's not shredding concrete
at Ocean Beach Skatepark, he's kicking through surf at
Imperial Beach or scarfing down fish tacos from the
nearest roadside shop. His wiry, six-foot frame can't
hide his live-or-die lifestyle — scars on his elbows, fresh
road rash on his knees, and a first-degree sunburn on
his nose. However, Omar's not afraid to show off these
"battle scars" — often wearing little more than a t-shirt,
board shorts, and a pair of black skate shoes. The
Bones Brigade and the SoCal surf culture have heavily
influenced his personal and skating style. At the park
or on the street, Omar is as clean, creative, and
inventive as they come.

STORY SETTING: West Coast

ABOUT TONY HAWK

TONY HAWK is the most famous and influential skateboarder of all time. In the 1980s and 1990s, he was instrumental in skateboarding's transformation from fringe pursuit to respected sport. After retiring from competitions in 2000, Tony continues to skate demos and tour all over the world.

He is the founder, President, and CEO of Tony Hawk Inc., which he continues to develop and grow. He is also the founder of the Tony Hawk Foundation, which works to create skateparks and empower youth in low income communities.

TONY HAWK WAS THE FIRST SKATEBOARDER TO LAND THE 900 TRICK, A 2.5 REVOLUTION (900 DEGREES) AERIAL SPIN, PERFORMED ON A SKATEBOARD RAMP.

ABOUT THE AUTHOR_

DONNIE LEMKE works as a children's book editor and writer in Minneapolis, Minnesota. He has written dozens of graphic novels, including the Zinc Alloy series and the adventures of Bike Rider. He also wrote *Captured Off Guard*, a World War II story, and a graphic novelization of *Gulliver's Travels*, both selected by the Junior Library Guild. Most recently, Lemke has written several chapter books for DC Comics.

AUTHOR Q & A_

Q: HAVE YOU PARTICIPATED IN ANY ACTION SPORTS? HOW HAVE THEY INFLUENCED YOU?

A: As a teenager, I skateboarded a little and probably got good enough to pop a decent ollie. But growing up on dirt roads in rural Minnesota didn't give me a whole lot of opportunity to practice outdoors. Instead, I spent A LOT of time honing my skills with a controller — playing *Skate or Die!* (talk about old-school) on Nintendo or *Tony Hawk's Pro Skater* for PS one.

Q: COULD YOU DESCRIBE YOUR APPROACH TO THE TONY HAWK'S 900 REVOLUTION SERIES?

A: When developing the idea for Tony Hawk's 900 Revolution, I was definitely influenced by books, video games, and movies I've watched. Specifically, manga, such as *Dragon Ball* and *Scott Pilgrim*, heavily influenced the quest aspect of TH900 Revolution. In *Dragon Ball*, a child named Goku searches for seven mystical objects. In *Scott Pilgrim*, the main character must destroy his girlfriend's seven evil exes. Like video games, both these books have strong objectives, which keep the reader engrossed until the very end. I'm hoping this series is just as addictive.

TONY HAWK'S 900 revolution

TONY HAWK'S 900 REVOLUTION, VOL. 1: DROP IN

Omar Grebes never slows down. When he's not shredding concrete at Ocean Beach Skatepark, he's kicking through surf or scarfing down fish tacos from the nearest roadside shop. Soon, his live-or-die lifestyle catches the attention of big-name sponsors. But one of them offers Omar more than he bargained for . . . a chance to become the first member of the mysterious 900 Revolution team and claim his piece of history.

TONY HAWK'S 900 REVOLUTION VOL. 2: IMPULSE

When you skate in New York, it's about getting creative, and fourtee year-old Dylan Crow conside himself a street artist. You wo catch him tagging alley wa Instead, he paints the streets with board. He wants to be seen grindi rails in Brooklyn and popping olli at the Chelsea Piers. But when Dyl starts running with the wrong crow his future becomes a lot less certa until he discovers the Revolutic

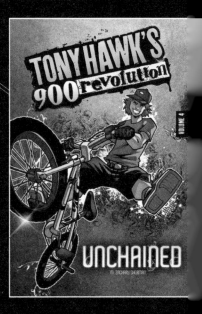

TONY HAWK'S 900 REVOLUTION, VOL. 3: FALL LINE

Amy Kestrel is a powder pig. Often hidden beneath five layers of hoodies, this bleach-blonde, CO ski bum is tough to spot on the street. However, get her on the slopes, and she's hard to miss. Amy always has the latest and greatest gear. But when a group of masked men threaten her mountain, she'll need every ounce of the one thing she lacks — confidence — and only

TONY HAWK'S 900 REVOLUTION, VOL. 4: UNCHAINED

Joey Rail learned to ride before could walk. He's tried every t wheeled sport imaginable, but always comes back to BMX freest The skills required for this da sport suit his personality. Joey is outdoor enthusiast and loves tak risks. But when he's approac by the first three members the Revolution, Joey must m a decision . . . follow the same

IMPULSE

. . . Nestled inside the wooden container, on top of several strips of newspaper insulation, sat the broken tail of an old skateboard. Splintered and frayed, the wooden kicktail still had part of its grip tape intact on top. However, the graphic on the bottom was almost scraped off from overuse. The Artifact measured three inches wide and six inches long.

"A broken skateboard deck! Really? Seriously? This is so stupid!" Dylan Crow pulled the Artifact out of the box and waved it in the air, upset and confused.

Detective Case gazed at Dylan's hand gripping the board piece and shaking it violently.

"Kid, look — look at your hand!" he said.

Dylan's face suddenly changed from anger to shock at what he saw.

A stream of electricity flowed over his hand. The strange energy enveloped it, making a slight crackling sound. It trickled out of the board and onto Dylan's fingers and palm.

"What is this?" asked Dylan.

The teen started to get scared.

He'd never seen anything or heard of anything like this before. The blue bolts leaped from fingertip to fingertip as he wiggled the broken board in his hands.

Smiling from ear to ear, Case tried to calm him.

"Kid, that's the Artifact!" he explained.

"What?" Dylan squeaked out.

"It likes you," said the detective. "I don't know why, but man does it like you!"

"That's great," said Dylan. "But what is it?"

Case shook his head and shrugged. "Seriously, we don't really know. I mean that? That's a kicktail from a broken skateboard. But the energy —? Some people think it's a key. One that, when assembled with all its other parts, will unlock some kind of power . . . . If those guys were to get their hands on it, who knows where it could end up. We can't let that happen!"

Quickly, Dylan placed the tailfin back in the box. He slammed the lid, locking the latch back in place.

The electricity promptly stopped.

"I don't care," he said and quickly handed the box to Detective Case.

Read more about Dylan Crow in the next adventure of . . .

Tony Hawk's 900 Revolution

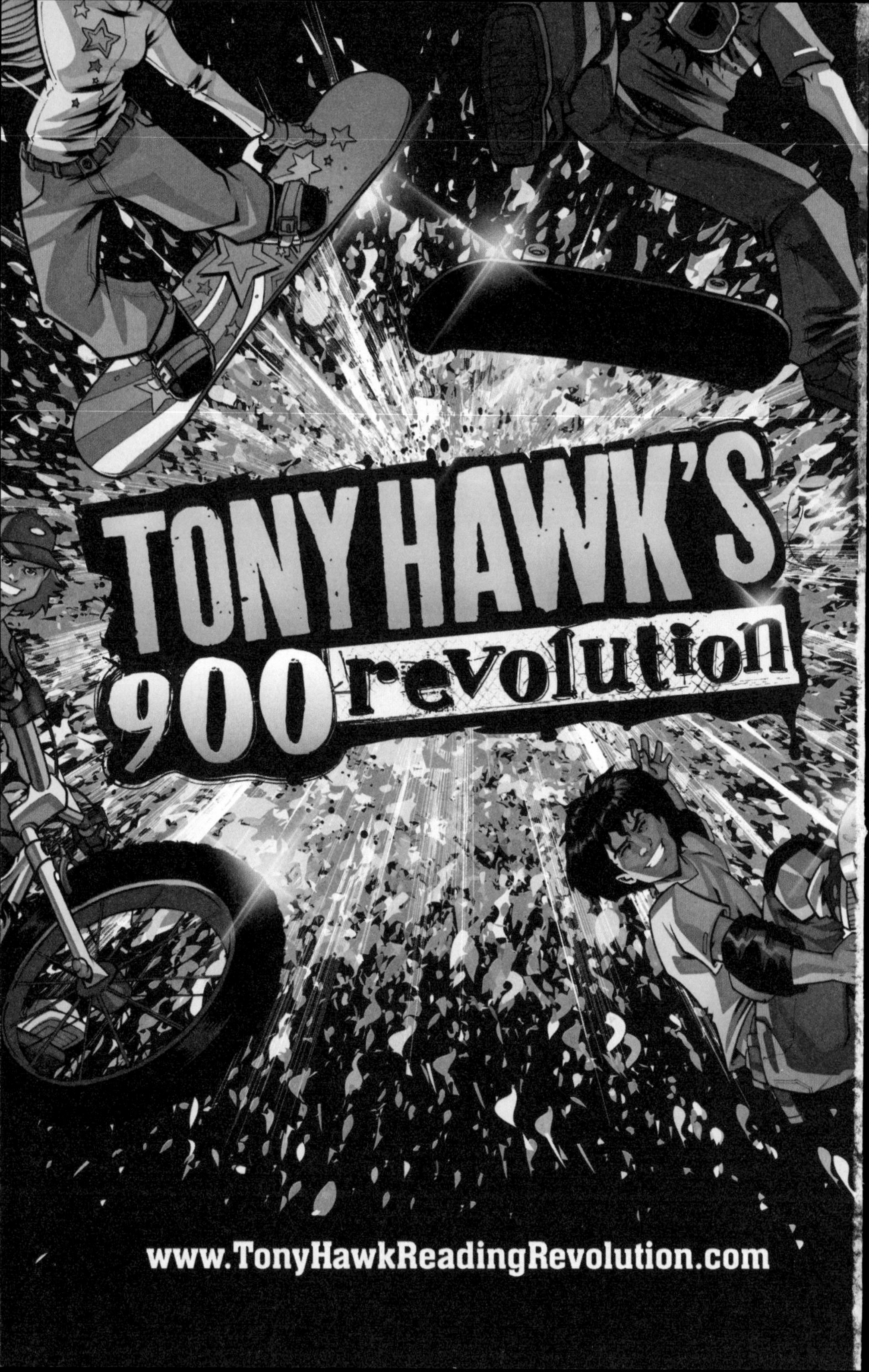
TONY HAWK'S
900 revolution
www.TonyHawkReadingRevolution.com